In the Footsteps of the Master

Walking With Christ Through the Holy Land

Contents

Editorial Director, James Kuse
Managing Editor, Ralph Luedtke
Production Editor/Manager, Richard Lawson
Photographic Editor, Gerald Koser

Written and Designed by
Ellen Hohenfeldt

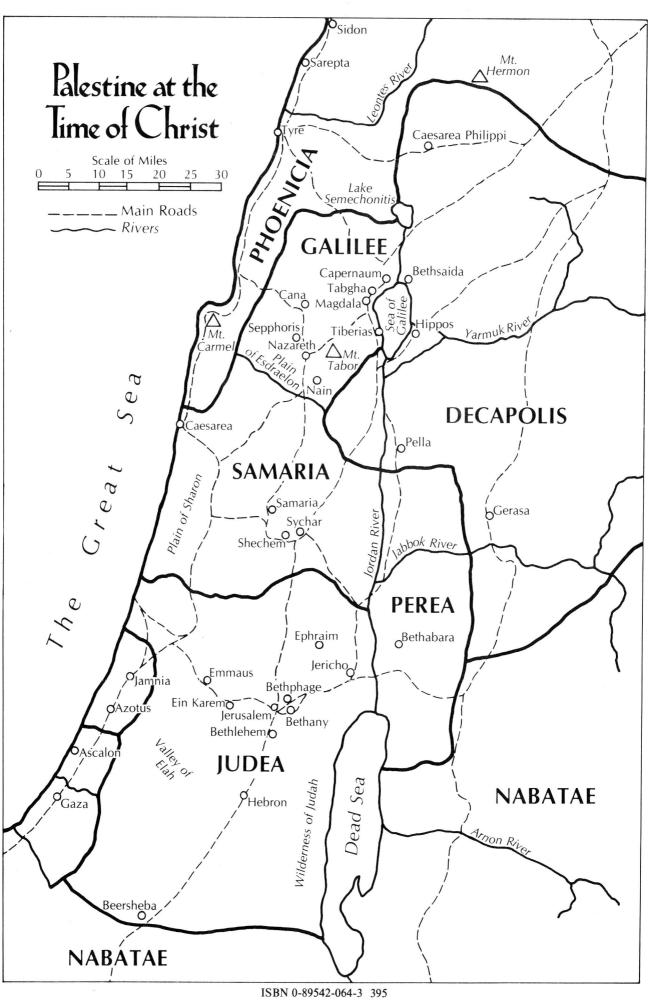

Palestine at the Time of Christ

Scale of Miles

0   5   10   15   20   25   30

– – – Main Roads

〜〜 Rivers

Sidon

Sarepta

Leontes River

Mt. Hermon

Tyre

Caesarea Philippi

PHOENICIA

Lake Semechonitis

GALILEE

Cana

Capernaum
Tabgha
Magdala

Bethsaida

Sea of Galilee

Hippos

Yarmuk River

Mt. Carmel

Sepphoris

Nazareth

Tiberias

Plain of Esdraelon

Mt. Tabor

Nain

DECAPOLIS

The Great Sea

Caesarea

Pella

SAMARIA

Plain of Sharon

Samaria

Sychar

Shechem

Gerasa

Jordan River

Jabbok River

PEREA

Ephraim

Bethabara

Jericho

Emmaus

Jamnia

Bethphage

Ein Karem

Jerusalem

Bethany

Azotus

Bethlehem

Ascalon

Valley of Elah

JUDEA

Hebron

Wilderness of Judah

Dead Sea

NABATAE

Gaza

Arnon River

Beersheba

NABATAE

ISBN 0-89542-064-3 395

IDEALS PUBLISHING CORP., MILWAUKEE, WIS. 53201
© COPYRIGHT MCMLXXVI, PRINTED AND BOUND IN U.S.A.

History of the Holy Land

During the long, troubled history of the Holy Land, some of the monuments built by Christians were destroyed, but many others are still standing. Each year thousands of pilgrims and tourists visit them. This book is a pilgrimage to the places and sights of Christ's homeland.

When Christ was born, Herod the Great was the Roman-appointed king of the Holy Land. One of the accomplishments of this self-serving tyrant was the rebuilding of the temple. The Wailing Wall, which may still be seen in the city, is part of the western wall of this temple, which is the same temple Christ knew.

After the death of Herod in 4 B.C., Palestine was divided between two of his sons. Herod Antipas ruled Galilee and Perea until 40 A.D. and Herod Archelaus ruled Judea and Samaria briefly. He was deposed in 6 A.D. After that time, his provinces were ruled by Roman procurators. One of the procurators of Judea was Pontius Pilate, who judged and sentenced Jesus.

During the Roman rule, the local inhabitants staged many rebellions until, in 69 A.D., Titus besieged the city. It lay in near ruins until the year 130 A.D. when Emperor Hadrian leveled what was left and built an entirely new city. In doing so, he desecrated Jewish and Christian shrines and built pagan ones in their places.

In 325, Constantine the Great conquered the land in the name of Christianity. His mother, Helena, toured the Holy Land searching for important Christian sites. Constantine then had great churches built there, including the Church of the Holy Sepulchre at the site of Christ's tomb.

In 614, amid great destruction, the Persians invaded the land. They were driven out shortly afterward by the Caliph Omar in 639. This began the Moslem occupation which lasted until 1917, nearly 1,300 years.

During these years, the Holy Land was claimed by Christianity only three times. This was during the Crusades, which began in 1096 and lasted over a period of almost two hundred years.

In the First World War, Palestine became a British protectorate. It remained in British hands until 1948 when the Israeli state was formed. The formation of Israel has not brought peace, however, and the Holy Land remains a troubled part of the world.

The Coming of Christ

He shall be great, and shall be called the Son of the Highest.

Luke 1:32

The Annunciation

Two thousand years ago, the city of Nazareth was a peaceful little hamlet. The town nestled in a valley amid fifteen gently sloping hills. Never an important religious center, Nazareth was not even mentioned in the Old Testament. All the large synagogues were in the neighboring city of Sepphoris, capital of Galilee. Here, reinforcements of the city were strengthened and a magnificent court built by Herod the Great, while Nazareth remained an undefended little country town. No wonder Nathanael saw fit to ask Philip: "Can there any good thing come out of Nazareth?" (John 1:46)

Yet it is Nazareth that was chosen by the Lord for an event which changed the world. It was here that the Angel Gabriel, speaking with the authority of God, greeted a young woman with the words: "Hail, thou that art highly favored, the Lord is with thee: blessed art thou among women." (Luke 1:28)

Mary was troubled and afraid, but the angel spoke again.

"Fear not, Mary: for thou hast found favor with God. And, behold, thou shalt conceive in thy womb, and bring forth a son, and shalt call his name Jesus. He shall be great, and shall be called the Son of the Highest; and the Lord God shall give unto him the throne of his father David: And he shall reign over the house of Jacob for ever; and of his kingdom there shall be no end." (Luke 1:30-33)

Inside the beautiful Church of the Annunciation, completed in 1969, one can still see the place where tradition has it the angel visited Mary. Mary's house was no more than a cave made larger by brick walls extending the front. At the back of the cave now stands an altar. The altarpiece depicts the scene of the Annunciation. Between two green lamps is a tablet with an inscription which reads: "Here the Word was made flesh."

Altar in the Church of the Annunciation at the site of the Virgin Mary's house, where the Angel Gabriel announced that she would become the mother of the Messiah. The two red granite columns mark the spots where Mary and the Angel stood. The inscription reads *Verbum Caro Hic Factum Est*—Here the Word was made flesh.

My soul doth magnify the Lord, and my spirit hath rejoiced in God my Saviour. For he hath regarded the low estate of his handmaiden: for, behold, from henceforth all generations shall call me blessed. For he that is mighty hath done to me great things; and holy is his name. And his mercy is on them that fear him from generation to generation. He hath showed strength with his arm; he hath scattered the proud in the imagination of their hearts. He hath put down the mighty from their seats, and exalted them of low degree. He hath filled the hungry with good things; and the rich he hath sent empty away. He hath holpen his servant Israel, in remembrance of his mercy; As he spake to our fathers, to Abraham, and to his seed for ever.

Luke 1:46-55

A mosaic on the Church of the Visitation shows
Mary on her way from Nazareth to Ein Karem, the
home of her cousin Elisabeth. In the courtyard of
the Church, the *Magnificat,* the song in which
Mary rejoiced at being chosen mother of our Lord,
is inscribed in forty-one languages.

And Mary arose in those days, and went into the hill country with haste, into a city of Juda. Luke 1:39

The Visitation

The pledge of Mary's future motherhood was the birth of John the Baptist to Zacharias and Elisabeth, Mary's aged cousin. Many places claim to be the site of this event, chief among them Ein Karem. In the Gospels, the place is not given a specific name. The only clue to the town's identity is the phrase in Luke: "And Mary arose in those days, and went into the hill country with haste, into a city of Juda; and entered into the house of Zacharias, and saluted Elisabeth." (Luke 1:39-40)

If Ein Karem is that "city of Juda," it has probably changed little since it saw the birth of John. It is a sleepy little village of cobblestone streets, surrounded by fertile valleys. A refreshing spring still in use gives the place its name, translated Vineyard Spring.

To this town, then, Mary hurried to see her cousin, who was filled with the Holy Spirit at the sight of her. Luke records the moving scene: "And she spake out with a loud voice, and said, Blessed art thou among women, and blessed is the fruit of thy womb. And whence is this to me, that the mother of my Lord should come to me? For, lo, as soon as the voice of thy salutation sounded in mine ears, the babe leaped in my womb for joy." (Luke 1:42-44)

The Church of the Visitation was built in the Byzantine era (fifth to sixth century). It is one of the most colorful in the Holy Land, marking the spot where the meeting may have occurred. The *Magnificat,* the song in which Mary rejoiced at being chosen mother of our Lord, is written in forty-one languages on plaques in the courtyard.

Mary stayed with and cared for Elisabeth for three months, until about the time of the birth of John. The relatives wanted to name the child Zacharias after his father, who had lost his power of speech. But Zacharias wrote on a tablet that the child's name was John. Immediately his speech was restored and he began to praise God. When the people saw this they were afraid, and said, "What manner of child shall this be? And the hand of the Lord was with him." (Luke 1:66)

Today, St. John's Church, also of the Byzantine era, stands at the site where the herald of the Messiah was born. An inscription on white marble proclaims: "This is the birthplace of the Forerunner of the Lord."

The city of Bethlehem, birthplace of Christ

And there were in the same country shepherds abiding in the field, keeping watch over their flock by night. And, lo, the angel of the Lord came upon them, and the glory of the Lord shone round about them; and they were sore afraid. And the angel said unto them, Fear not; for, behold, I bring you good tidings of great joy, which shall be to all people. For unto you is born this day in the city of David a Saviour, which is Christ the Lord. And this shall be a sign unto you; Ye shall find the babe wrapped in swaddling clothes, lying in a manger. And suddenly there was with the angel a multitude of the heavenly host praising God, and saying, Glory to God in the highest, and on earth peace, good will toward men.

Luke 2:8-14

Shepherds still tend their flocks in the Holy Land, just as they did on the day when three shepherds watching flocks outside Bethlehem were the first to hear the news of the birth of Christ.

...nd she brought forth her ...rstborn son, and wrapped ...im in swaddling clothes, ...nd laid him in a manger.
...uke 2:7

The Nativity

Unlike Nazareth, Bethlehem is often mentioned in the Old Testament. It was here that Ruth gleaned barley while she lived with her mother-in-law, Naomi. Here also, David was born, tended his flocks, and was anointed king by Samuel. Of this small town, the prophet Micah said: "But thou, Bethlehem Ephratah, though thou be little among the thousands of Judah, yet out of thee shall he come forth unto me that is to be ruler in Israel; whose goings forth have been from of old, from everlasting." (5:2)

Bethlehem was probably a stopping place for many travelers. About four miles away was the Herodium, Herod's palace. This stands on a high hill, at the foot of which is a village accessible only through Bethlehem. The Herodium was the administrative center for all places south of Jerusalem.

The town would have been full of visitors during the imperial census for which Joseph and Mary came to register. This explains why there was no room at the inn. The couple proceeded to a stable, where Mary gave birth to the baby Jesus. Here the shepherds came to view the Child.

The Church of Nativity stands at the spot where, according to tradition, Jesus was born. It was built by the Emperor Constantine and his mother Helena in the year 325. It is the oldest Christian church in the world that is still in use. Built in the shape of a cross, it looks like a fortress from the outside. In a niche in the Grotto of the Nativity stands a marble altar. On the floor beneath the altar is a marble slab in which is imbedded a silver star inscribed with the words: "Here Jesus Christ was born of the Virgin Mary."

Arise, and take the young child and his mother, and flee into Egypt.

Matthew 2:13

The Flight

The family carefully followed the Jewish traditions. After eight days, they had the Baby circumcised and named Him Jesus, according to the Angel Gabriel's command. Then, at the end of forty days, they took the Child to Jerusalem where He was presented at the Temple. The family returned to Bethlehem rather than home to Nazareth.

Herod heard the rumors that a new King had been born. Out of jealousy, he decided to slay all the male children in Bethlehem two years old and younger. But the family had been forewarned: "Behold, the angel of the Lord appeareth to Joseph in a dream, saying, Arise, and take the young child and his mother, and flee into Egypt, and be thou there until I bring thee word: for Herod will seek the young child to destroy him." (Matthew 2:13)

And so the Holy Family took the long and arduous caravan route through the Sinai Desert to Egypt, where they stayed "until the death of Herod." (Matthew 1:15)

Many believe that this is the rock cave in which
the Holy Family dwelt in Nazareth, and where
Jesus grew to manhood.

And the child grew, and waxed strong in spirit . . . and the grace of God was upon him. Luke 2:40

The Early Years

Jesus lived in Nazareth until He was about thirty years old. During the years in which He grew from child to man, He probably learned Joseph's trade, carpentry. He must also have gone to the town synagogue to receive His education.

The streets of Nazareth have changed little since Christ's time. They are narrow, paved alleys with gutters in the middle, and are lined with dark, cavernous little shops and open-air markets. Perhaps Jesus helped His mother draw water from the city's only well, which still runs today.

The Gospels are vague about this period in the life of Christ, but one event is described in detail: When Jesus was twelve, the family made its regular pilgrimage to Jerusalem at Passover. On the way back, his parents discovered that Jesus was not in the company. They turned back. "And it came to pass, that after three days they found him in the temple, sitting in the midst of the doctors, both hearing them, and asking them questions. And all that heard him were astonished at his understanding and answers. And when they saw him, they were amazed: and his mother said unto him, Son, why hast thou thus dealt with us? behold, thy father and I have sought thee sorrowing. And he said unto them, How is it that ye sought me? wist ye not that I must be about my Father's business?" (Luke 2:46-49)

The streets of Nazareth have been narrow and crowded since the days when Jesus walked here. Men, women, children and even burros floo the alleyways

Baptism

The historic Jordan River winds its way through much of the length of the Holy Land. From its source, high in the snows of Mt. Hermon, it runs to the Dead Sea, 1,200 feet below sea level. The total drop is more than 2,300 feet, making the Jordan valley the deepest in the world.

John's favorite place for baptisms was the Jordan. His mission was quite successful. Crowds came from all around to hear John preach, confess their sins and be baptized.

One day, Jesus appeared at the banks of the Jordan. "And it came to pass in those days, that Jesus came from Nazareth of Galilee, and was baptized of John in Jordan. And straightway coming up out of the water, he saw the heavens opened and the Spirit like a dove descending upon him: and there came a voice from heaven, saying, Thou art my beloved Son, in whom I am well pleased." (Mark 1:9-11)

Later, Jesus was standing on the banks of the Jordan when He received John's disciples, sent from Machaerus where John was imprisoned. They asked the question: "Art thou he that should come? or look we for another?" (Luke 7:19) Jesus' answer: "Go your way, and tell John what things ye have seen and heard; how that the blind see, the lame walk, the lepers are cleansed, the deaf hear, the dead are raised, to the poor the gospel is preached. And blessed is he, whosoever shall not be offended in me."

And it came to pass in those days, that Jesus came from Nazareth of Galilee, and was baptized of John in Jordan. Mark 1:9

The site on the River Jordan where according to tradition Jesus was baptized by John.

Overleaf: The desolate Wilderness of Judah, where Jesus fasted and was tempted by the devil.

Fasting and Temptation

After being baptized by John, Jesus withdrew into the wilderness to fast and meditate. According to tradition, Jebel-Quarantal is the Mountain of the Temptation where He fasted for forty days and forty nights. This barren, craggy peak rises a thousand feet above the plain of Jordan. Halfway up, a Greek monastery clings to the mountainside, marking the supposed spot where He was first approached by the devil.

The view from the mountain is exceptionally beautiful. The heights overlook the Jordan valley, with the green river winding its way through the plain, flanked by white hills. To the east lies Jericho, an oasis in the desert, with its lush citrus groves. Stretched across the southern horizon is the blue surface of the Dead Sea. On its western shore lie the rolling brown hills of the Wilderness of Judah. Showing Jesus this beautiful landscape, Satan tempted Him the third time: "All these things will I give thee, if thou wilt fall down and worship me." (Matthew 4:9)

The Wedding at Cana

Cana is significant as the sight of Christ's first miracle, but its location is disputed. Many scholars fix the spot at what is now Kefr Kenna, about three miles northeast of Nazareth. This pleasant little Arab town contains the only spring for twenty miles around. Assuming that this is the Cana of the Bible, then this must be the very spring from which the water was drawn that Jesus turned into wine.

Today, a Franciscan church stands at the site of the bridegroom's house, to which Mary, as well as Jesus and His disciples, were invited to celebrate the wedding. There were evidently more guests than anticipated, and the wine began to run out. Mary turned to Jesus and softly said: "They have no wine." (John 2:3) His answer: "Woman, what have I to do with thee? mine hour is not yet come." (John 2:4) But Mary said to the stewards: "Whatsoever he saith unto you, do it." Jesus had them fill six jugs with water and take them to the governor of the feast, who found them filled with wine. "This beginning of miracles did Jesus in Cana of Galilee, and manifested forth his glory; and his disciples believed on him." (John 2:11)

The Mount of the Temptation is also called Jebel-Quarantal (forty) after the forty days and nights Jesus fasted there. From the peak Satan offered Him "all the kingdoms of the world, and the glory of them." (Matthew 4:8) A Greek monastery can barely be discerned clinging to slopes to the left of center in the photograph.

And he was there in the wilderness forty days, tempted of Satan . . . and the angels ministered unto him. Mark 1:13

The Ministry

The Woman of Samaria

With the wedding at Cana, Christ's ministry was begun. John records that soon afterwards He went to Jerusalem to celebrate Passover, but was angry and disappointed when He found "in the temple those that sold oxen and sheep and doves, and the changers of money sitting: and when he had made a scourge of small cords, he drove them all out of the temple, and the sheep, and the oxen; and poured out the changers' money, and overthrew the tables; and said unto them that sold doves, Take these things hence; make not my Father's house a house of merchandise." (2:14-16)

For sometime after Passover He stayed in the area. At about this time, too, He had a conversation with Nicodemus, the Pharisee, and tried to make him see that he must be reborn "of water and of the Spirit" in order to see the kingdom of God. (John 3:5)

But soon He decided to return to Galilee. His route took Him through Samaria, where He stopped at Jacob's well and had the famous conversation with the woman of Samaria. "Give me to drink," He said. The woman was surprised. The Samaritans, a mixture of Jewish and Gentile races, had long been spurned as heretics by the Jews. Hence her response: "How is it that thou, being a Jew, askest drink of me, which am a woman of Samaria?" Jesus, trying to reveal His true identity to her, said: "If thou knewest the gift of God, and who it is that saith to thee, Give me to drink; thou wouldest have asked of him, and he would have given thee living water." But the woman did not understand, even after He revealed that He knew all about her life, facts He could not have guessed. Finally, she said: "I know that Messias cometh, which is called Christ: when he is come, he will tell us all things." And Jesus said, "I that speak unto thee am he." (John 4:3-26)

Even today, in many parts of the Holy Land women must go to the well to fetch water. It was such a woman as this, perhaps carrying a water jug on her head, that Jesus met at Jacob's Well in Samaria.

24

There cometh a woman of Samaria to draw water: Jesus saith unto her, Give me to drink. John 4:7

The synagogue at Capernaum, where Jesus often
taught. Now in ruins, the synagogue was
once a stately building beautifully decorated
with carvings.

Rejection at Nazareth

Jesus' decision to return to His hometown of Nazareth ended in failure. On the Sabbath, He went to the small synagogue and got up to read. He read from Isaiah: "The Spirit of the Lord is upon me, because he hath anointed me to preach the gospel to the poor; he hath sent me to heal the broken-hearted, to preach deliverance to the captives, and recovering of sight to the blind, to set at liberty them that are bruised, to preach the acceptable year of the Lord." (Luke 4:18-19) All eyes were on him as he stopped reading, handed away the scroll, seated himself and said: "This day is this Scripture fulfilled in your ears." (Luke 4:21) The people were amazed. They could not believe that one from their own town, the son of a carpenter, whom they had known since he was a little boy, could be applying the words of Isaiah to himself. "Is not this Joseph's son?" they asked in amazement. (Luke 4:22)

Outraged, they carried him out of the city to a hill in order to throw him down. But Jesus, "passing through the midst of them, went his way." (Luke 4:30) And so, He became an example of his own words, that "No prophet is accepted in his own country." (Luke 4:24)

And he came to Nazareth . . . and, as his custom was, he went into the synagogue on the sabbath day, and stood up for to read.
Luke 4:16

Fishermen ply the Sea of Galilee which has
yielded abundant catches since the time
of Christ.

And Jesus said unto them, Come ye after me, and I will make you to become fishers of men.
Mark 1:17

Galilee

Much of Christ's public ministry centered around the Sea of Galilee. Here He chose some of His disciples, preached the Sermon on the Mount, fed the five thousand, and performed many other miracles and healings.

Today the bright blue lake has an austere beauty. It lies six hundred feet below sea level, rimmed by gently rolling, barren hills.

But in the time of Christ, the lake must have been the scene of much more activity. Its fertile shores and perfect climate nourished acres of orchards. Walnut, palm, olive and fig trees all flourished there. Today, efforts are being made to restore the land to its former fruitfulness.

Then, as now, the lake teemed with fish. At least forty different types of freshwater fish may be caught there. One of these is known as St. Peter's fish. It has an unusually large mouth in which the male carries the eggs and young. Some believe this is the kind of fish Peter hooked according to Jesus' instructions, and found a coin in its mouth for tribute money.

Circling the lake are the ruins of many cities which were bustling when the area was more densely populated. The eastern shores were Gentile country. Gerasa, Gadara, Hippos and Scythopolis were all Greek cities. Just across the lake, on the western shore, was Tiberias, a city with a Roman flavor. Indeed, Tiberias was built and named by Herod Antipas, Tetrarch of Galilee, as a compliment to the reigning Caesar. Also on the west side of the lake was Magdala, home of Mary Magdalene.

The town most significant in the ministry of Christ was Capernaum. In those days it was a trading center, with a customs house and large marketplace. Barges were loaded in the harbor to carry produce to the other side of the lake. In the midst of this bustling city, Jesus made a headquarters for his ministry.

And leaving Nazareth, he came and dwelt in Capernaum, which is upon the sea coast. Matthew 4:13

Capernaum

Jesus taught more and performed more miracles in Capernaum than anywhere else. Time and again, He would tour the area, preaching and healing, and then return to Capernaum, where He probably stayed at the house of Simon Peter. Here He healed Peter's mother-in-law of a fever (Matthew 8:14-15), raised from the dead the daughter of Jairus, the ruler of the synagogue (Mark 5:21-24, 35-43), and healed the servant of a Roman centurion. (Matthew 8: 5-13)

Many believe the ruined synagogue which may still be seen at Capernaum is the very one Christ used for His teaching. What remains is a curious mixture of classical Corinthian columns and carved stones decorated with flowers, trees, grapes and other emblems. These are placed upon the paved courtyard of what must have been a very richly ornamented building.

All the while He was at Capernaum, Christ's fame and word of His miracles were spreading. At one point, the crowds besieging Him became so great that He was forced to withdraw into the wilderness. When He returned to Capernaum, word was immediately passed that He was home, and the crowds soon became so thick that one man, carried on a pallet by four others, could not get near Him. "And when they could not come nigh unto him for the press, they uncovered the roof where he was: and when they had broken it up, they let down the bed wherein the sick of the palsy lay. When Jesus saw their faith, he said unto the sick of the palsy, Son, thy sins be forgiven thee." (Mark 2:4-5) But some of the onlookers perceived this statement as blasphemy, and wondered who but God could forgive sins. Jesus answered them: "Why reason ye these things in your hearts? Whether is it easier to say to the sick of the palsy, Thy sins be forgiven thee; or to say, Arise, and take up thy bed, and walk? But that ye may know that the Son of man hath power on earth to forgive sins, (he saith to the sick of the palsy,) I say unto thee, Arise, and take up thy bed, and go thy way into thine house. And immediately he arose, took up the bed, and went forth before them all; insomuch that they were all amazed, and glorified God, saying, We never saw it on this fashion." (Mark 2:8-12)

The Church of the Beatitudes stands on a h
north of the Sea of Galilee, commemorating
Sermon on the Mou

And they said, We have no more

but five loaves and two fishes.

Luke 9:13

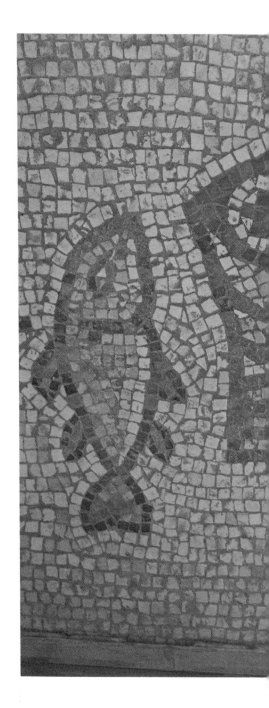

The Sermon on the Mount

As Jesus' reputation grew, so did His opposition. His enemies were constantly watching Him, trying to find some sort of accusation. Incidents such as the one above, where they accused Him of blasphemy when He cured the sick of the palsy, were becoming more frequent.

One day, on His way back from the Passover feast at Jerusalem, He passed through a wheat field where His disciples plucked the wheat and ate it. "And certain of the Pharisees said unto them, Why do ye that which is not lawful to do on the sabbath days? And Jesus answering them said, Have ye not read so much as this, what David did, when himself was ahungered, and they which were with him; how he went into the house of God, and did take and eat the showbread, and gave also to them that were with him; which it is not lawful to eat but for the priests alone? And he said unto them, That the Son of man is Lord also of the sabbath." (Luke 6:2-5)

On a Sabbath soon after, He healed a man with a withered hand, saying to the objectors: "I will ask you one thing; Is it lawful on the sabbath days to do good, or to do evil? to save life, or to destroy it?" (Luke 6:9) And the evangelist reports, "they were filled with madness; and communed one with another what they might do to Jesus." (Luke 6:11)

So it was that the opposition to His ministry grew so strong in Capernaum that He was forced to preach by the seashore outside the city. Calling His disciples to Him, He went to a nearby mountain. There He prayed all night long, and in the morning chose the twelve apostles "that they should be with him, and that he might send them forth to preach, and to have power to heal sicknesses, and to cast out devils." (Mark 3:14-15) Then He went to where the crowds had gathered from all over Palestine and preached the Sermon on the Mount. This most beautiful sermon contains some of the most beloved passages in the Gospels, including the Lord's Prayer and the Beatitudes.

A mosaic in the Basilica of Loaves and Fishes near Capernaum. The two fishes and basket of bread symbolize the miracle of the feeding of the five thousand.

Miracle of Multiplication

About two miles from Capernaum, at Tabgha (seven springs), stands the Basilica of the Loaves and Fishes. Built in the Byzantine period, the church contains world-renowned mosaics symbolizing the miracle of the feeding of the five thousand. Historically, this event took place on the east side of the lake, but tradition has moved the site to Tabgha.

One of the mosaics is a pavement depicting twenty-two different types of local birds. Before the church was built, the pavement was in the open air. When visitors came, a caretaker would brush the coarse sand from the mosaic, then spill water on it to bring out the colors. Amazingly, the ancient artwork survived this treatment and is now safely housed in the church.

Another of the mosaics shows a basket of bread, each loaf marked with a cross, flanked by two fish. Jesus took this amount of food, divided it up among the crowd which had come to hear Him preach, and then told His disciples to gather up the leftovers. "Therefore they gathered them together, and filled twelve baskets with the fragments of the five barley loaves, which remained over and above unto them that had eaten." (John 6:13)

The multitudes were impressed by the miracle and Jesus had a hard time getting away. He retired to a mountain to be alone while the disciples got a boat and began to row across the sea to Capernaum. Suddenly, they saw Him walking on the sea toward them. They were afraid but He quieted their fears. When they took Him into the boat, they were immediately at their destination.

The crowd caught up with Jesus at the synagogue in Capernaum. He accused them of being interested "not because ye saw the miracles, but because ye did eat of the loaves, and were filled." (John 6:26) He told them they should concern themselves more with spiritual things. "Labor not for the meat which perisheth, but for that meat which endureth unto everlasting life, which the Son of man shall give unto you." (John 6:27) He spoke of a different kind of bread which is Christ Himself, but to partake of it they must have faith. He thereby promised the Lord's Supper. "I am the living bread which came down from heaven: if any man eat of this bread, he shall live for ever: and the bread that I will give is my flesh, which I will give for the life of the world . . . Verily, verily, I say unto you, Except ye eat the flesh of the Son of man, and drink his blood, ye have no life in you. Whoso eateth my flesh, and drinketh my blood, hath eternal life; and I will raise him up at the last day." (John 6:51-54)

A sower went out to sow his seed: and as he sowed, some fell by the wayside; and it was trodden down, and the fowls of the air devoured it. And some fell upon a rock; and as soon as it was sprung up, it withered away, because it lacked moisture. And some fell among thorns; and the thorns sprang up with it, and choked it. And other fell on good ground, and sprang up, and bare fruit a hundredfold. And when he had said these things, he cried, He that hath ears to hear, let him hear. Now the parable is this: The seed is the word of God. Those by the wayside are they that hear; then cometh the devil, and taketh away the word out of their hearts, lest they should believe and be saved. They on the rock are they, which, when they hear, receive the word with joy; and these have no root, which for a while believe, and in time of temptation fall away. And that which fell among thorns are they, which, when they have heard, go forth, and are choked with cares and riches and pleasures of this life, and bring no fruit to perfection. But that on the good ground are they, which in an honest and good heart, having heard the word, keep it, and bring forth fruit with patience.

Luke 8:5-15

Threshing in the Holy Land today is done in the ancient manner. A pronged fork is used to toss the wheat in the air. The wind separates the wheat from the chaff.

Tyre and Sidon

Jesus emphasized that He had come to save first the "lost sheep of the house of Israel." (Matthew 15:24) Therefore He seldom left His own country. Now, however, He crossed the border into Phoenicia to the coastal cities of Tyre and Sidon. News of His teachings and miracles had spread to this area long before He arrived. Some of the residents of these two commercial cities had been present to hear Him preach the Sermon on the Mount. (Luke 6:17)

Both of the cities were centers of commerce in the time of Christ. Tyre was built on two islands which were later connected to the mainland by a causeway. It had two harbors, one facing south to Egypt, the other north to Sidon. The town was important for producing purple dye which was obtained from snails caught in the Mediterranean Sea. Coinage was imperative in this center for world trade, and Tyre had the right to produce its own. One of its issues, a silver shekel, was the type of coin paid to Judas.

On His way north from Tyre, Jesus stopped at Sarepta, now called Sarafand, a glass-blowing center. It is here that a "woman of Canaan" approached Him with the plea: "Have mercy on me, O Lord, thou son of David; my daughter is grievously vexed with a devil." (Matthew 15:22) Jesus heard her appeal and said "O woman, great is thy faith: be it unto thee even as thou wilt." (Matthew 15:28)

Twenty miles north of Tyre lies Sidon, the modern Saida. This was the most important trading city on the coast. Jesus must have seen slaves in the busy harbor loading ships with the products of the area—purple cloth, glassware and other valuables. Ships from all over the world arrived to empty their cargoes of silk, precious metals, wines.

The modern town of Saida bears no resemblance to the glittering city upon whose ruins it is built. The harbors are silted up and no longer used for shipping. Nearby are the ruins of Kalat el-Bahr, a medieval crusader fortress.

The medieval Crusader fortress called Kalat el-Bahr (Castle of the Sea) is near Sidon. In the foreground is the ruined stone bridge by which the fortress was reached.

*Then Jesus went thence, and departed
into the coasts of Tyre and Sidon.
Matthew 15:21*

The Church of the Transfiguration on the peak of Mount Tabor.

Caesarea Philippi

Jesus' travels in the north took Him to Caesarea Philippi. Near here, He asked His disciples who the people were saying He was. "Some say that thou art John the Baptist; some, Elias; and others, Jeremias, or one of the prophets," they answered. (Matthew 16:14) To Jesus' next question, "But whom say ye that I am?" Simon Peter answered "Thou art the Christ, the Son of the living God." (Matthew 16:15-16)

"And Jesus answered and said unto him, Blessed art thou, Simon Bar-jona: for flesh and blood hath not revealed it unto thee, but my Father which is in heaven. And I say also unto thee, That thou art Peter, and upon this rock I will build my church; and the gates of hell shall not prevail against it." (Matthew 16:17-18)

Now Jesus would concentrate less on teaching the multitudes and turn to instructing His disciples. The days of His public ministry were growing short. "From that time forth began Jesus to show unto his disciples, how that he must go unto Jerusalem, and suffer many things of the elders and chief priests and scribes, and be killed, and be raised again the third day." (Matthew 16:21)

The Transfiguration

And his face did shine as the sun, and his raiment was white as the light. Matthew 17:2

Six days after leaving Caesarea Philippi, Jesus took three of His most faithful disciples to the top of a "holy mountain." There He was transfigured before them. According to long tradition, the mountain was Tabor. Rising almost two thousand feet above the flat plain of Esdraelon, Tabor can be seen from as far away as Nazareth. From the summit, the view includes snow-capped Mount Hermon to the north, the shimmering blue Sea of Galilee to the east, and across Samaria, Mount Carmel on the Mediterranean.

The top is usually reached by a footpath which twists its way up the slopes from Daberath, now called Daburiyeh, at the foot of the mountain. Here, Jesus left nine of the disciples, then undertook the hour-long climb with Peter, James and John. After spending the night in prayer, He was transfigured, "And his face did shine as the sun, and his raiment was white as the light." (Matthew 17:2) Christ appeared with two other figures, Moses and Elijah. The disciples were amazed, and Peter said to Jesus, "Lord, it is good for us to be here: if thou wilt, let us make here three tabernacles; one for thee, and one for Moses, and one for Elias." (Matthew 17:4) But while he was still speaking, a bright cloud overshadowed them and God spoke: "This is my beloved Son, in whom I am well pleased; hear ye him." (Matthew 17:5) The disciples fell on their faces in fear, but Jesus told them to rise. When they looked up again, He was alone.

The first church at the top of Mt. Tabor, built by the Empress Helena in the fourth century, was called the Church of St. Saviour. Another was built near the ruins of the first during the turmoil of the Crusades. The present Church of the Transfiguration was completed in 1924 and stands at the site of the Church of St. Saviour. Part of an ancient confessional unearthed during excavations is preserved in the crypt of the church.

Dawn and dusk fill the church with a beautiful glow which illuminates mosaics showing the transfigured Christ. In the background are Moses and Elijah; in the foreground, the amazed figures of Peter, John and James. On either side of the main entrance are chapels dedicated to Moses and Elijah, fulfilling Peter's suggestion.

Soon after they came down from the mountain after the transfiguration, Jesus said to His disciples: "The Son of man shall be delivered into the hands of men." (Luke 9:44) The time of His struggle was near at hand.

Feast of the Tabernacles

During the Feast of the Tabernacles, Jesus returned to Jerusalem. The situation was very tense. The scribes and Pharisees were constantly testing Him. At one point, they sent officers to arrest Him, but they returned empty-handed. When asked why they had not brought Jesus, they answered: "Never man spake like this man." (John 7:46)

Trying to find evidence against Him, the scribes and Pharisees produced a woman accused of adultery, saying that according to the law her crime was punishable by stoning. Jesus' answer to them was: "He that is without sin among you, let him first cast a stone at her." (John 8:7) Later, He spoke again: "I am the light of the world: he that followeth me shall not walk in darkness, but shall have the light of life." (John 8:12)

On a Sabbath soon afterward, Jesus passed a man who had been blind from birth. He spat on the ground to make a clay which He rubbed on the man's eyes, saying, "Go, wash in the pool of Siloam . . . He went his way therefore, and washed, and came seeing." (John 9:7) When the incident was investigated, the man refused to deny that Jesus was the Son of God, saying, "If this man were not of God, he could do nothing." (John 9:33) The Pharisees cast the man out. Jesus said: "For judgment I am come into this world, that they which see not might see; and that they which see might be made blind." (John 9:39)

Go, wash in the pool of Siloam . . . He went his way therefore, and washed, and came seeing. John 9:7

The pool of Siloam, to which Jesus sent the blind man. After washing in the waters, he could see. It is fed by a spring which runs through a channel 1,750 feet long. The channel was cut by King Hezekiah (eighth century B.C.).

And when he thus had spoken, he cried with a loud voice, Lazarus, come forth. And he that was dead came forth. John 11:43-44

Lazarus Raised

Not far from Jerusalem, on the southeast slope of the Mount of Olives, is Bethany. This was the home of Mary, Martha and Lazarus whom Jesus loved and often visited. When Lazarus died, the sisters sent word to their friend. His disciples tried to convince Jesus not to go back to that dangerous territory, but when they saw He would not be dissuaded, it was Thomas who said: "Let us also go, that we may die with him." (John 11:16)

When Martha heard that Jesus was coming, she ran to meet Him. Jesus told her her brother would rise again, to which she answered, "I know that he shall rise again in the resurrection at the last day." (John 11:24) But this is not what Jesus meant. He told her: "I am the resurrection, and the life: he that believeth in me, though he were dead, yet shall he live: and whosoever liveth and believeth in me shall never die. Believest thou this?" (John 11:25-26) Martha confessed her absolute faith: "Yea, Lord: I believe that thou art the Christ, the Son of God, which should come into the world." (John 11:27)

Mary joined them and the three, followed by other mourners, proceeded to the grave of Lazarus, now four days dead. There Jesus was moved and wept. The people said, "Behold how he loved him!" (John 11:36)

Jesus told them to remove the stone. After a prayer He called Lazarus forth. "And he that was dead came forth, bound hand and foot with graveclothes; and his face was bound about with a napkin. Jesus saith unto them, Loose him, and let him go. Then many of the Jews which came to Mary, and had seen the things which Jesus did, believed on him." (John 11:44-45)

The word of this miracle spread far and wide. Some of the witnesses went to the Pharisees and told what they had seen. The Pharisees gathered together in council to decide what to do, knowing that if they let Jesus alone everybody would soon believe in Him. "Then from that day forth they took counsel together for to put him to death." (John 11:53)

The tomb of Lazarus in Bethany, where Jesus called "Lazarus, come forth," and his friend rose from the dead

Overleaf: Jerusalem from the Mount of Olives. On
Palm Sunday, Jesus viewed the city from this peak
and wept over it. The golden dome to the right in
the picture is the Mosque of Omar, which stands
at the site of the temple.

And when he was come near, he beheld the city, and wept over it.
Luke 19:41

Perean Ministry

The result of the meeting of the Pharisees amounted to a warrant for Jesus' arrest. He left the Jerusalem area, first going to Ephraim with His disciples. Then He crossed the Jordan into Perea for the last stage of His public ministry.

Even in Perea the Pharisees tried to trap Jesus into some indiscretion or blasphemy. Some of them questioned Him about the Jewish divorce laws. In this case, Jesus who had been accused of taking the law too lightly, was even more strict than Moses had been. Traditional Jewish law permitted a husband to divorce his wife whenever "she find no favour in his eyes, because he hath found some uncleanness in her." (Deuteronomy 24:1) But Jesus said that in marriage two people become one. "What therefore God hath joined together," He said, "let not man put asunder." (Matthew 19:6)

Some of Jesus' admirers brought little children to Him in hopes that He would bless them. His disciples, undoubtedly aware of the tension He had been under, tried to send them away. "But when Jesus saw it, he was much displeased, and said unto them, Suffer the little children to come unto me, and forbid them not, for of such is the kingdom of God. Verily I say unto you, Whosoever shall not receive the kingdom of God as a little child, he shall not enter therein. And he took them up in his arms, put his hands upon them, and blessed them." (Mark 10:14-16)

On His way back to Jerusalem, Jesus went through Jericho, where a large crowd had gathered to see Him pass by. Among them was Zaccheus, a small man who climbed a sycamore tree to get a better view. When Jesus saw him there, He said, "Zaccheus, make haste, and come down; for today I must abide at thy house." (Luke 19:5) This surprised the people. Zaccheus was the chief tax collector in the area, and tax collectors were notoriously dishonest. They received no salary but often became rich by collecting more in taxes than the government required. But Zaccheus had repented of his previous dishonesty, and said, "Behold Lord, the half of my goods I give to the poor; and if I have taken any thing from any man by false accusation, I restore him fourfold. And Jesus said unto him, This day is salvation come to this house." (Luke 19:8-9)

Jesus continued on His way to Jerusalem, stopping again in Bethany at the home of Mary, Martha and Lazarus where He ate supper. After the meal, Mary anointed Jesus' feet with a costly ointment, prompting Judas to ask why it was not sold and the money given to the poor. According to John, Judas said this "not that he cared for the poor; but because he was a thief, and had the bag, and bare what was put therein. Then said Jesus, Let her alone: against the day of my burying hath she kept this. For the poor always ye have with you, but me ye have not always." (12:6-8)

Suffer the little children to come unto me. Mark 10:14

Villagers walk down a road in Bethany where Christ
often visited His friends Mary, Martha and Lazarus.

The Way of the Cross

And a very great multitude spread their garments in the way; others cut down branches from the trees, and strewe them in the way. Matthew 21:8

Palm Sunday

Approaching Jerusalem, He passed near Bethphage where He told two of His disciples to bring the donkey they would find there. Mounted on the donkey, He rode to the Mount of Olives, escorted by joyous crowds who scattered palm branches and garments in His path. But their joy was not His. Viewing the city from the heights, Jesus wept over it and pronounced the solemn words: "If thou hadst known, even thou, at least in this thy day, the things which belong unto thy peace! but now they are hid from thine eyes. For the days shall come upon thee, that thine enemies shall cast a trench about thee, and compass thee round, and keep thee in on every side, and shall lay thee even with the ground, and thy children within thee; and they shall not leave in thee one stone upon another; because thou knewest not the time of thy visitation." (Luke 19:42-44)

The view of Jerusalem from the Mount of Olives is one of the finest even today. In the foreground can be seen the old city, dotted with the golden domes of churches. The large, modern city rises in the background. The spot where Jesus may have stood is commemorated by the chapel of Dominus Flevit, which means "The Lord Wept."

The Golden Gate marks the spot of the old Zusa gate through which Jesus entered Jerusalem c Palm Sunday. The Golden Gate has been walle up since the ninth centur

And the chief priests and the scribes sought how they might take him by craft, and put him to death. Mark 14:1

In Jerusalem

After His triumphant entry into Jerusalem, Jesus spent several days going to the Temple to preach and heal the sick. Meanwhile, His enemies continued to try to trap Him into exposing Himself. At one point they asked Him what He thought about paying taxes. "What thinkest thou? Is it lawful to give tribute unto Caesar, or not?" (Matthew 22:17) But Jesus knew they were trying to trap Him. "Why tempt ye me, ye hypocrites? Show me the tribute money. And they brought unto him a penny. And he saith unto them, Whose is this image and superscription? They say unto him, Caesar's. Then saith he unto them, Render therefore unto Caesar the things which are Caesar's; and unto God the things that are God's. When they had heard these words, they marvelled, and left him, and went their way." (Matthew 22:18-22)

Time and again they tried to trap Him. Finally, seeing He would not compromise Himself, the chief priests and elders met in the house of Caiaphas, acting high priest, to plan some strategy. They decided to wait until the feast day was over, and then kill Jesus. Judas went to them and said "What will ye give me, and I will deliver him unto you? And they covenanted with him for thirty pieces of silver. And from that day on he sought opportunity to betray him." (Matthew 26:15-16)

The section of Jerusalem known as the Old City
This is the city Christ knew

And as they were eating, Jesus took bread, and blessed it . . . and said, Take, eat; this is my body. Matthew 26:26

The Last Supper

"Now was the first day of the feast of the unleavened bread" (Matthew 26:17) and Jesus and the disciples prepared to eat the Passover supper. In a large upper room in a house on Mount Zion, the apostles and their Master assembled. When everyone had arrived, Jesus took a towel and a basin of water and began to wash the disciples' feet. This was ordinarily the job of the lowliest servant, and Peter was ashamed to have his Master wash his feet. Jesus told him that, although he could not yet fully appreciate the significance of the act, he would understand it later. Peter still objected: "Lord, thou shalt never wash my feet. Jesus answered him, If I wash thee not, thou hast no part with me." (John 13:8) Jesus' answer indicated that the washing was a symbol not only of His humility, but also of a spiritual cleansing.

It was on this same evening that, as He had so often intimated He would, Jesus established the Lord's Supper. But first He exposed Judas: "Verily I say unto you, that one of you shall betray me." (Matthew 26:21) The disciples looked anxiously at one another, wondering who was guilty. Jesus said, "He it is, to whom I shall give a sop, when I have dipped it." (John 13:26) So He dipped the morsel and gave it to Judas, saying, "That thou doest, do quickly," (John 13:27) and Judas immediately got up and left the room to do his work.

Next, taking up the unleavened bread according to the ancient Jewish ritual for the feast, He spoke the new words: "Take, eat; this is my body. And he took the cup, and gave thanks, and gave it to them, saying, Drink ye all of it; for this is my blood of the new testament, which is shed for many for the remission of sins." (Matthew 26:26-28)

Long tradition points to the Cenacle on Mount Zion as the scene of the Last Supper. This building was reportedly already a church in the year 135 A.D. Since then it has changed hands many times. In the sixteenth century it was occupied by Franciscans who had built a beautiful church on the site. The Franciscans were expelled by Moslems, who made a mosque of the upper room. In 1948, Mount Zion became Israeli territory and the Moslems left. The many changes of ownership have taken their toll on this place where Christ gave the first communion.

Mount Zion near the southwest corner of the Jerusalem city wall. The Church of the Dormition stands beside the "upper room" in which the Last Supper was celebrated.

I am the true vine, and my Father is the husbandman. Every branch in me that beareth not fruit he taketh away: and every branch that beareth fruit, he purgeth it, that it may bring forth more fruit. Now ye are clean through the word which I have spoken unto you. Abide in me, and I in you. As the branch cannot bear fruit of itself, except it abide in the vine; no more can ye, except ye abide in me. I am the vine, ye are the branches. He that abideth in me, and I in him, the same bringeth forth much fruit: for without me ye can do nothing. If a man abide not in me, he is cast forth as a branch, and is withered; and men gather them, and cast them into the fire, and they are burned. If ye abide in me, and my words abide in you, ye shall ask what ye will, and it shall be done unto you. Herein is my Father glorified, that ye bear much fruit; so shall ye be my disciples. As the Father hath loved me, so have I loved you: continue ye in my love. If ye keep my commandments, ye shall abide in my love; even as I have kept my Father's commandments, and abide in his love. These things have I spoken unto you, that my joy might remain in you, and that your joy might be full.

John 15:1-11

Many varieties of grapes grow in the Holy Land, reminiscent of Christ's parable of the true vine told to the apostles on the night of the Last Supper.

Gethsemane

From the Last Supper, Jesus and the disciples crossed the Valley of Kidron to Gethsemane. The name means oil press, and eight ancient olive trees still grow there. Some say they were present to witness Christ's agony.

On Byzantine and Crusader remains stands the Basilica of the Agony, also known as the Church of All Nations. A large piece of rock which was found in the older building has been preserved in the new church. Many believe this is the rock on which Christ sweated blood before meeting His captors.

Taking with Him His three closest disciples, Peter, James and John, Jesus asked them to keep watch while He drew apart to pray: "O my Father, if it be possible, let this cup pass from me: nevertheless not as I will, but as thou wilt." (Matthew 26:39)

Twice He found His disciples asleep and twice he told them to watch. But the third time He said "Sleep on now, and take your rest: it is enough, the hour is come; behold, the Son of man is betrayed into the hands of sinners." (Mark 14:41) And while He spoke a crowd approached led by Judas. Judas kissed Him, thereby identifying Him to His captors. Jesus allowed Himself to be arrested without offering resistance while the disciples fled in all directions.

Then cometh Jesus with them unto a place called Gethsemane, and saith unto the disciples, Sit ye here, while I go and pray yonder.
Matthew 26:37

Then took they him, and led him, and brought him into the high priest's house. Luke 22:54

The Trial of Jesus

Jesus' official trial did not begin right away. From Gethsemane He was taken to the house of Caiaphas, the high priest. There they questioned Him about His disciples and His doctrine, to which Christ answered, "Why askest thou me? ask them which heard me, what I have said unto them: behold, they know what I said." (John 18:21) Thus, with dignity, Jesus protested His innocence. When one of the officers present struck Him, asking how He dared speak to the high priest like that, Jesus answered simply: "If I have spoken evil, bear witness of the evil: but if well, why smitest thou me?" (John 18:23) Meanwhile, in the courtyard outside the house, Peter denied His master three times, fulfilling Christ's prophecy.

The next day, the Sanhedrin assembled. This was the highest religious body of the land, presided over by Caiaphas. Witnesses were called. According to the law, the testimony of at least two of them had to agree in order to prove guilt.

The testimonies of the first witnesses were declared invalid. There is no record of what these testimonies were. Then Jesus was accused of saying that He would destroy the temple and build it again in three days. But this evidence was also thrown out because the witnesses could not agree. Jesus said nothing to defend Himself through the whole proceeding. Finally the high priest could stand it no longer. He spoke to Jesus, saying, "Answerest thou nothing? what is it which these witness against thee?" (Mark 14:60) Still Jesus held His peace. And then Caiaphas asked the decisive question: "Art thou the Christ, the Son of the Blessed? And Jesus said, I am: and ye shall see the Son of man sitting on the right hand of power, and coming in the clouds of heaven." (Mark 14:61-62)

The case was closed. Jesus was guilty of calling Himself the Messiah and that was blasphemy. "What need we any further witnesses?" Caiaphas asked. (Mark 14:63) They all agreed He was guilty and should be condemned to death.

Under the large dome in the picture opposite lie the Lithostratos, the stone courtyard of the fortress Antonia, where Jesus was judged by Pontius Pilate. The smaller dome to the right belongs to the Chapel of the Condemnation

And Pilate gave sentence that it should be as they required.
Luke 23:24

The pavement on which Christ was judged by Pilate. Some of the rocks still bear markings made by soldiers who wiled away the hours on watch. Some of the markings are just designs; some were used for a game like tic-tac-toe.

Jesus Before Pilate

Since it was against the law for the Jews to put any man to death, the religious leaders could not pass the death sentence themselves. For this they must go to Pilate, the Roman procurator. Although the real reasons they wanted Jesus put to death were religious, they knew Pilate would have nothing to do with a case of that kind. So when he asked them the charges they brought against Him they gave political ones: "We found this fellow perverting the nation, and forbidding to give tribute to Caesar, saying that he himself is Christ a king." (Luke 23:2) These accusations were false. For instance, it is nowhere recorded that Jesus ever told the people not to pay taxes.

Pilate then spoke to Jesus himself. "Art thou the King of the Jews?" (John 18:33) To this Jesus answered: "Thou sayest that I am a king. To this end was I born, and for this cause came I into the world, that I should bear witness unto the truth. Everyone that is of the truth heareth my voice." (John 18:37)

Pilate could find no fault with Him and would have released Him, but the crowd would not let Him go. Upon learning that Christ was from Galilee, Pilate sent Him to Herod, governor of Galilee. Luke records that Herod was glad to see Jesus. Having heard of the marvelous things He had done, Herod hoped to see some miracle performed by Him. But Jesus disappointed him, and would not speak a single word. So Herod only mocked Him and sent Him back to Pilate.

The officers who received Jesus also mocked Him and struck Him and put a crown of thorns on His head. Jesus was a pitiable sight when Pilate brought Him out to show the people, saying, "Behold the man!" (John 19:5) Pilate, still reluctant to give the order for crucifixion, offered to release Him, as it was customary to release one prisoner during the festival. The crowd called for the release of Barabbas, who had been imprisoned for murder and insurrection. When Pilate asked what he should do with Jesus, "they cried out again, Crucify him." (Mark 15:13) In the end, Pilate relented. "And Pilate gave sentence that it should be as they required." (Luke 23:24)

The place where Pilate sat in judgment was the Lithostratos, a courtyard outside the Roman Fortress of Antonia. In Jerusalem today, a pavement of huge stones can still be seen. Many believe this to be the actual site on which Christ was judged and condemned to death.

Then delivered he him therefore unto them to be crucified. And they took Jesus, and led him away. John 19:16

The Crucifixion

The sentence was executed immediately after it was handed down. Jesus was taken out of the city, bearing His own cross until He stumbled and fell from weakness. Then Simon of Cyrene was ordered to carry the cross for Him. Tradition has it that the Via Dolorosa was the route they took that day to Calvary, to Golgotha or the place of the skull. Today, the route is retraced by Christians from all over the world, who follow Jesus' steps to the cross every Friday.

"And when they came to the place, which is called Calvary, there they crucified Him" (Luke 23:33), along with two robbers, one on either side. At the top of the cross, in mockery, was placed a sign in three languages bearing the words "Jesus of Nazareth the King of the Jews."

At the foot of the cross the soldiers cast lots for His clothes. Many others were gathered there in sorrow during Jesus' last hours, including His mother, Mary Magdalene and John the apostle, to whom Christ tenderly entrusted His mother.

"And the sun was darkened, and the veil of the temple was rent in the midst. And when Jesus had cried with a loud voice, he said, Father, into thy hands I commend my spirit." (Luke 23:45-46) And then, at about three o'clock on a Friday afternoon, He died.

The Via Dolorosa, the street down which Christ walked on the way to the cross.

And Jesus answered them, saying, The hour is come, that the Son of man should be glorified. Verily, verily, I say unto you, Except a corn of wheat fall into the ground and die, it abideth alone: but if it die, it bringeth forth much fruit. He that loveth his life shall lose it; and he that hateth his life in this world shall keep it unto life eternal. If any man serve me, let him follow me; and where I am, there shall also my servant be: if any man serve me, him will my Father honor. Now is my soul troubled; and what shall I say? Father, save me from this hour: but for this cause came I unto this hour. Father, glorify thy name. Then came there a voice from heaven, saying, I have both glorified it, and will glorify it again. The people therefore that stood by, and heard it, said that it thundered: others said, An angel spake to him. Jesus answered and said, This voice came not because of me, but for your sakes. Now is the judgment of this world: now shall the prince of this world be cast out. And I, if I be lifted up from the earth, will draw all men unto me.

John 12:23-32

The rooftop of the Church of the Holy Sepulchre
The Church is erected over the traditional site of
Christ's tomb. It was built by crusaders

And when Jesus had cried with a loud voice, he said, Father, into thy hands I commend my spirit. Luke 23:46

The Burial

Since the body could not be left upon the cross overnight, Joseph of Arimathea received permission from Pilate to take charge of it. With Nicodemus, another rich man and secret follower of Jesus, Joseph took the body to his own tomb hewn out of rock nearby. There they prepared it with spices, wrapped it in clean linen and laid it on a rock. Then they went out and sealed the opening with a large stone.

What many believe to be the actual tomb of Christ now lies carefully guarded in the Church of the Holy Sepulchre. The tradition linking the tomb in the church with Christ's burial place is very old. The Emperor Constantine had the original Church of the Holy Sepulchre erected in the year 325. This majestic basilica was modeled after St. Peter's in Rome. It displayed both the tomb and the nearby rock of Calvary on which Christ was crucified. However, like so many ancient buildings in the Holy Land, Constantine's church was meant for destruction. In 614, it was crushed by the Persians. Crusaders picked up the pieces and built a new Romanesque church on the site, but this too was shaken by wars and earthquakes. Now the patched and crumbling building must be supported by huge steel beams in order to keep from collapsing. Still, the five denominations that own the church carefully stand watch over the sacred places it contains.

The Latin Chapel in the Church of the Holy Sepulchre marks the spot where Jesus was crucified, or nailed to the cross.

Surely he hath borne our griefs, and carried our sorrows: yet
we did esteem him stricken, smitten of God, and afflicted.
But he was wounded for our transgressions, he was bruised
for our iniquities: the chastisement of our peace was upon
him; and with his stripes we are healed. All we like sheep
have gone astray; we have turned every one to his own
way; and the Lord hath laid on him the iniquity of us all.
He was oppressed, and he was afflicted, yet he opened not
his mouth: he is brought as a lamb to the slaughter, and as
a sheep before her shearers is dumb, so he openeth not his
mouth. He was taken from prison and from judgment: and
who shall declare his generation? for he was cut off out of
the land of the living: for the transgression of my people
was he stricken.

Isaiah 53:4-8

Burial chamber in the Holy Sepulchre containing
the rock ledge on which the body of Chris
was laid

And after this Joseph of Arimathaea . . . besought that he might take away the body of Jesus. John 19:38

Why seek ye the living among the dead? He is not here, but is risen. Luke 24:5-6

The Resurrection

The tomb of Christ is significant not only as the Lord's burial place but as the scene of His Resurrection. It was to this spot that the women were hurrying on Easter Sunday, carrying with them spices to anoint the body and wondering who would roll the stone away for them. It was here they were surprised to find the stone already rolled away. And here they found not the dead body of their Lord but an angel, who asked them: "Why seek ye the living among the dead? He is not here, but is risen: remember how he spake unto you when he was yet in Galilee, saying, The Son of man must be delivered into the hands of sinful men, and be crucified, and the third day rise again." (Luke 24:5-7)

That the body was gone was a fact that even Jesus' enemies could not deny. They tried to explain it by saying the disciples had stolen the body while the guards were sleeping. In fact, they bribed the soldiers themselves to spread this rumor.

But the angel told the women the real meaning of the empty tomb: "He is risen." It was with "fear and great joy" that they ran to tell the disciples the great news as the angel had instructed them. At first the disciples were skeptical. They went to inspect the tomb and wondered what had happened. But before long they had more proof: not only the testimony of the women, but the word of Christ Himself.

Inside the Chapel of the Angel, so called because this was where Mary discovered the angels instead of the body of Christ. Originally, it was a large outer room, apart from the burial chamber itself where mourners could gather. The low door at the back leads to the burial chamber

The Appearances

Christ appeared several times after the Resurrection. On the same day the tomb was found empty, two disciples were walking to their home in Emmaus near Jerusalem, sadly discussing the events of the day, when they were joined by a stranger. They invited Him home for supper and at the meal they found their guest was Christ Himself.

On another occasion He appeared to Peter and other disciples on the Sea of Galilee at Tabgha. They were fishing and having no luck when they saw Jesus standing on the shore. He told them to cast their nets once more. They did so and this time their nets were full. On the shore they shared a meal with Christ, at which time He charged Peter with the mission to "Feed my lambs . . . Feed my sheep . . . Feed my sheep." (John 21:15-17)

Through these appearances, Jesus convinced His followers that He was truly resurrected. They believed what they saw and told others.

And, behold, two of them went that same day to a village called Emmaus. Luke 24:13

Emmaus, about eight miles from the city of Jerusalem. After His Resurrection, Jesus appeared to two disciples walking to their homes in this town.

Overleaf: The Sea of Galilee, near the place where Christ appeared to the disciples after the Resurrection.

*But when the morning was now come, Jesus stood on the shore:
but the disciples knew not that it was Jesus. John 21:4*

While he blessed them, he was parted from them, and carried up into heaven. Luke 24:51

The Ascension

Jesus remained on earth for forty days after the Resurrection, appearing to His disciples and giving them final instructions. At the end of this period, He led them out of the city to the Mount of Olives near the spot where He had paused and wept over Jerusalem on Palm Sunday.

Gathering His disciples around Him, Jesus ordered them to spread the gospel: "Go ye therefore, and teach all nations, baptizing them in the name of the Father, and of the Son, and of the Holy Ghost: teaching them to observe all things whatsoever I have commanded you: and, lo, I am with you always, even unto the end of the world." (Matthew 28:19-20) "And it came to pass, while he blessed them, he was parted from them, and carried up into heaven" (Luke 24:51) ". . . and a cloud received him out of their sight." (Acts 1:9)

The first Church of the Ascension was built at the site in 470 A.D. by a pious and wealthy Roman woman. It was a beautiful octagonal structure, with open arches on all sides. It so impressed the Moslems that the Mosque of Omar, which now stands at the site of the Temple of Jerusalem, was modeled after it in the seventh century. In 614, the Church of the Ascension fell to the Persians. It was nearly in ruins when the crusaders rebuilt it, preserving the footprints of Christ—the legendary last traces of Him before He ascended from the world of men.

The Mount of Olives, from which Jesus is said to have ascended into heaven.

Characteristic of the Holy Land is the striking combination of old and new. Here, at the Wailing Wall, the shofar or sacred trumpet is still blown on High Holy Days.

For even hereunto were ye called: because Christ also suffered for us, leaving us an example, that ye should follow his steps: Who did no sin, neither was guile found in his mouth: Who, when he was reviled, reviled not again; when he suffered, he threatened not; but committed himself to him that judgeth righteously: Who his own self bare our sins in his own body on the tree, that we, being dead to sins, should live unto righteousness: by whose stripes ye were healed. For ye were as sheep going astray; but are now returned unto the Shepherd and Bishop of your souls.

1 Peter 2:21-25

Index

*All scripture quotations are
from the King James Version.*